# John Doe
## ? - February 28, 2012

### B. Heather Mantler

*One day...*

He stopped at the wall and looked at the generic painting. The fields were merely brush strokes of yellow and brown to him. The scene as a whole was foreign to him as a cheap hotel room. He turned and walked back across the room. This side had an electric fireplace, but there were no reason for it to be turned on today. He stopped and glanced at his wristwatch.

She was late, he thought to himself as he turned back around and started across the room again.

Half-way across there came a knock at the door. He stopped and headed for the apartment door. Reaching it, he hesitated a moment. He reminded himself that it could not be Melissa at the door, but his gut told him it was not the woman he was waiting for.

The thought came up that he should ask the manager to put in a peephole. With a few hundreds slipped to him, the manager wasn't likely to even ask why.

The man took the chain off the door before turning the knob. He opened the door enough he could see who was there and still have enough time to slam it shut. There were three men standing outside the door. Two of the men were in suits and the one in a navy uniform of a police officer. The man opened the door wider.

"Can I help you?" the man asked.

"Are you John Smith?" the man in the suit on the right asked as he held up a police badge.

"Yes," the man answered.

"You're under arrest for murder," the other detective said bringing out a set of handcuffs.

The man stood there as the detective put the handcuffs on him. Then he was led out by the detectives. They led him around the corner of the hallway. The elevator and the hallway in front of it were blocked up with yellow crime scene tape.

As the police led the man toward the stairs, he glanced at the scene with disinterest before going back to concentrating on where he was being led.

*A couple hours later...*

The detective stared at the officer and the lab technician.

"You're telling me, the man in there, has no fingerprints, and no face or DNA in any database?" the detective asked pointing to the man on the other side of the glass.

"The whole palm of his hand has been burned," the officer said, "We can't get fingerprints or palm prints."

"We checked every database and couldn't find a match to his DNA," the lab technician said, "So, we ran his picture against all the databases and there were no results."

"So, all we know about this guy is that his name is John Smith," the detective said, "And we only know that because it was the name on the apartment lease. He could be anyone."

"We'll see if we can't narrow that down," the lab technician said, "We will check his clothes and the apartment."

"John Smith did ask that his lawyer be called," the

officer said, "He hasn't said anything about not talking." The officer offered a business card to the detective. The detective took the card and looked at it. The detective recognized the lawyer's name. He was a good lawyer and a good guy. He had worked for the prosecution many times. He didn't have a list of scumbag clients, nor did he like to represent people like that.

"Call him," the detective said handing the business card back. Then the detective headed for the interrogation room.

*A minute later...*

He tapped his fingers on the table. The clock ticked on the wall behind him. Somewhere in the distance there were echoes of men yelling at each other. A large black fly was repeatedly attacking the bare light bulb that hung over him.

A mirror encompassed the wall in front of him. It reflected the metal table that was bolted to the floor, the two chairs build for practicality not comfort, and bare grey walls.

Tick, buzz, bam, bam, tick, bam, buzz, tick, tap, tap, tick, bam, tap, tick, buzz, tap, bam, tick.

He stopped tapping the table and smoothed his hair back with that hand. He watched the mirror to check that every strand was in place. He dropped his hand back to the table. He lifted his finger to start tapping again.

The door opened and the detective stepped inside before closing the door behind him. The detective had a file and an envelope in his hand. The detective set them on the table before sitting down in the opposite chair. The detective straightened the file folder before picking up the envelope and pouring the contents on the table. The items scattered themselves across its surface. The detective shook the envelope again just to make sure that everything was on the table.

"What happened, John?" the detective asked, "Who was she? And why did you shove her down the elevator shaft?"

"I didn't shove her down the elevator shaft," he replied. He stopped himself from reaching for the rusted screw that had come to rest near his hand. He looked at the detective rather than the objects.

"So, what happened?" the detective asked.

He glanced at the objects on the table before looking back at the detective.

"She used to be my mistress," he said, "I opened the apartment door to find her standing there. She was not supposed to be there because I told her the relationship was over two days ago. I asked her how she got passed the doorman and she said she had come through the basement window." He pushed the screws into a pile.

"Why did she show up?" the detective asked.

"She wanted our relationship to continue," he answered, "She said she would tell my wife about us if I refused. She was going to take the pictures of us to my wife as proof of the relationship." He picked up the slip of paper from the photo store. "She said the photos were hidden somewhere safe."

"What happened next?" the detective asked.

"I explained again to her that the relationship was over as I escorted her back to the elevator," he answered, "I gave her the keychain and nun figurine as gifts because I knew she collected religious items. She tried to give me the cologne, but I refused it. It was cologne she enjoyed the smell of and not the kind I usually wear."

"Did you go to a photographer for the photographs?" the detective asked picking up the business card.

"No," he answered, "She was a model. The card probably from her latest job."

"So, you are standing in front of the elevator doors," the detective said, "What happened?"

"We weren't at the elevator yet," he answered, "The apartment was on the other side of the building from the elevator. We were talking as we walked. When we came into view of the elevator, I saw the doors were open and slowed down. She didn't. She was angry at me and still was threatening me. She said that if I didn't keep seeing her then she was going to tell my wife."

"They must have been doing work on the elevator because there was an extension cord on the floor in front of the elevator. She wasn't looking where she was going and tripped over the cord. She fell into the elevator shaft. The elevator must have been on the basement floor."

"And you just walked away?" the detective asked.

"I figured the repairman would find her and report it," he said, "Then she wouldn't be connected back to me."

"Through the doorman we connected her to you," the detective said, "What was her name?"

"Melissa," he answered, "We never told each other our last names and I never tried to figure out what hers was."

"Did she call you John?" the detective asked.

"Yes," he answered.

"Does your wife call you John?" the detective asked.

"You can direct the rest of your questions to my attorney," he answered.

*Half an hour later...*

The detective was standing beside his desk reading a file when the lawyer entered the police station. The lawyer went over to the detective.

"How are you, Detective?" the lawyer asked offering his right hand.

"Well, how about yourself?" the detective shook hands with the lawyer.

"I just got back from a week off," the lawyer answered.

"Stay at home and relax, or get away for awhile?" the detective asked.

"My in-laws were having a family reunion," the lawyer answered, "The good times last about three days and then the rest of the time is waiting until we can come home."

"At least you get three days," the detective said.

"True," the lawyer said, "How is my client?"

"He gave us his story, but he won't tell us anything about who he is," the detective answered, "What do you know about him?"

"Not much," the lawyer answered, "All his bills are sent to John Smith, all cheques are signed John Smith, but his name isn't John Smith. I don't know what his name is and he isn't willing to tell me."

"I'm surprised he has a lawyer," the detective said.

"A former mistress was suing him for child support," the lawyer said, "He hired me to prove the child wasn't his, which only took a DNA test. I think he has had a vasectomy, but he won't admit to anything that might require giving out information about himself."

"Well, we can't find him in any database," the detective said, "Fingerprints, DNA, and photo came up with nothing."

"What is he in for?" the lawyer asked, "The officer didn't specify."

"Pushing his latest mistress down on elevator shaft," the detective answered.

"My guess," the lawyer said, "is that he broke up with her and she wasn't interested in letting go. He killed her because she inconvenienced him. Now he is hoping to deal with this and move on with his life."

"The charges aren't going away," the detective said.

'I know," the lawyer said, "He's in the interrogation room?"

"Yes," the detective answered. The lawyer headed into the back.

*The next day...*

The lab technician came into the police station and went over to the detective's desk. The detective looked up at him.

"What did you find?" the detective asked.

"Nothing as to who he could be," the lab technician answered, "His clothes don't hold any clues and the apartment is for the most part clean."

'For the most part?" the detective asked.

"The bed has plenty of DNA samples on it," the lab technician answered, "It looks like it hasn't been washed for the length of time that John Smith has been renting the apartment. We found his DNA as well as the woman from the elevator. There was newer female DNA sample and several older female DNA samples."

"Well, that answers what he had the apartment for," the detective said, "Anything useful?"

"No," the lab technician answered, "No matched in any database."

"Anything else?" the detective asked.

"There was a message from another lab," the lab technician answered, "John Smith's DNA is a match to an unsolved case that didn't come up in our search. The lab is going to send over the case file as soon as possible."

"Did they tell you anything about this case?" the detective asked.

"The victim is currently known only as Jane Doe number 1387692," the lab technician answered, "The DNA is never been matched to any missing person. Despite finding the body within twenty-four hours of the murder, they can't get fingerprints or use facial reconstruction. The person who called warned me about the case, something about the fact that every bone in the woman's body had been broken without her being crushed with something heavy."

"That doesn't sound good," the detective said.

"I'll bring the case file over as soon as I get it," the lab technician said.

"Thank you," the detective said. The lab technician turned and left the police station.

*The next morning…*

The lab technician entered the police station and took the file over the detective. The lab technician didn't say anything, he just left the file with the detective. After flipping through the report, the detective reached the pictures. For the first time in his fifteen years as a police officer, he lost his lunch over crime scene photos. According to the report, John Smith's DNA was all over the murder weapon as well as the body.

*Two months have passed…*

The television screen flickered once before it came up with the bright blue screen. The prosecution put the video tape into the VCR. The screen flickered again before the blue was replaced by a fairly clear picture of an apartment building hallway. It was empty of people, but the elevator door was open and there was a cord stretched out in front of it. A moment of empty hallway went by before John Smith and Melissa Russell came into view. There was no sound coming from the television. John had Melissa's elbow in a tight grip as he led her down the hallway. She didn't look happy and kept trying to twist away, but he wasn't letting go. They looked to be arguing with each other. Melissa didn't notice that they were headed for an open elevator shaft until she was on the edge. John shoved her forward. She could not keep her balance and fell. John stood there and looked over the edge. Then he nodded to himself before turning around and going back down the hallway. He walked out of the frame looking like nothing had happened. The prosecution stopped the tape and ejected it from the VCR before turning off the television.

*Three weeks later…*

The jury entered the court room in a single file line. They went to their seats and sat down. Finally they had all entered and the guard had closed the door. Everyone else was already settled and waiting. The judge waited until the jury was ready.

John was about the only person in the whole courtroom who was relaxed. His lawyer wanted to snap at him and get him to quit the self-confident attitude. The lawyer knew John was not going to get out of here scot-free. But he remained silent because that was what was needed at this time.

"Madam Foreman, have you reached a verdict?" the judge asked. The jury foreman stood up.

"Yes, your honour," she answered, "We the jury find the accused guilty of first degree murder in the cases of Melissa Russell and Jane Doe number 13878692."

"Thank you," the judge said, "The sentencing hearing will be tomorrow at ten o'clock." The judge banged the gavel against the base.

"All rise," the court clerk called. Everyone in the courtroom got to their feet. The judge stood up and left the courtroom. The lawyer didn't look at John as he collected all the papers and put them away in his briefcase. The sheriff came over to put the handcuffs back on John. John said nothing and went willingly. The lawyer glanced up at him as he was being led away. John had remained calm and still had that confident air. The lawyer shook his head as he got ready to leave the courtroom.

*The next morning...*

The lawyer sat there at the table as he waited. The sheriff brought John in and they went to the table. The sheriff undid the handcuffs before moving away. John gave off a calm air, but it was not as relaxed today.

"We can appeal," the lawyer told John, "I can have the process started immediately after this hearing is finished."

"Will that change the outcome of this whole process?" John asked.

"With the evidence the prosecution has," the lawyer replied, "not likely."

"Then there is no other point to appealing aside from wasting everyone's time?" John asked.

"Well, there are small chances things will change," the lawyer answered, "Most people try."

"I have no interest in wasting time," John said, "Do not bother with appealing."

"Okay," the lawyer said.

"All rise," the court clerk said. Everyone in the court room stood up. The judge came into the courtroom and sat down in his chair. The rest of the people took their seats.

"This is the sentencing hearing of John Smith," the court clerk announced, "Case number 736958." The court clerk sat down.

"John Smith," the judge said.

"Yes, your honour," John stood up.

"A jury of your peers has found you guilty of two counts of first degree murder," the judge said, "Due to the severity of the crimes, I sentence you to death. Do you have a method you prefer?"

"Lethal injection," John answered.

"You are hereby sentenced to death by lethal injection," the judge banged the gavel on the base.

*Two years later...*

John set the tray down before sitting down in the chair. He inhaled through his nose and sighed in contentment. John picked up his utensil and started to eat.

The poached eggs were cooked to the point where the yolks weren't runny, but still retained their flavour. There was no excess water on them, either. The eggs were as perfect as the ones he had been served at the diner he stopped at four years ago. If it hasn't been for his car troubles he would have bypassed the diner completely. But he was starving and his car was going to take an hour or two so he went inside. He had wiped off the seat before he sat down, wiped off the table before the waitress came over with the menu, and wiped off the cutlery before his food arrived. But the poached eggs had turned out to be perfect.

The bacon was crisp without being burnt. The pieces were still dripping with grease. They reminded him of the first night he had spent at his girlfriend's house. She had made him bacon and eggs the next morning. She had over-cooked the bacon that morning. She had blamed him for distracting her. That morning he hadn't minded over-cooked bacon.

The hash-browns were under salted, but he left the ketchup packets alone that were on the tray. It was better to have under salted hash-browns than desecrate them with ketchup. He had hated ketchup since the incident in high school. The person he had considered his best friend has dumped a container of ketchup over his head right in front of the girl he had a crush on. She declined his invitation to the school dance, even after he cleaned up. The whole episode was in the yearbook. He wished there were salt packets provided rather than ketchup packets. That would make more sense to him.

The toast might have been crisp at some point before the butter was slathered on. He put the toast to one side of the tray and focused his attention on the pancakes. The pancakes tasted wonderful. Completely unlike his mother's pancakes used to be. His mother's pancakes always tasted like backing powder despite having blueberries in them. But he never dared to say anything and he always ate them as if he loved them. He didn't have much of a choice at that point in his life.

The door opened and the chaplain entered the room before the door closed behind him. The chaplain smiled at John.

"How is your meal?" the chaplain asked coming to sit down across the table from John.

"Are you here to pray for my soul or to find out my name?" John asked.

"Merely to sit with you until it is time," the chaplain answered, "As I always do with inmates who are waiting for execution."

"I have no more interest in talking to you as I have any other time you have come to see me," John said.

'Then we can just sit here in quiet while we wait," the chaplain said.

*Two days after...*

The detective joined the lawyer, who was standing in the cemetery looking at John's grave stone. The two men stood without speaking. There were a flock of song birds in a tree to their left and somewhere out of sight there was a lawn mower in use. The sun was warm enough to keep the autumn chill away.

"Your office told me where to find you," the detective said.

"Another case?" the lawyer asked.

"No, I just wondered if you had figured out who he was." The detective gestured towards the grave stone. "I can't imagine how his wife feels. He went to work one morning and hasn't come home yet."

"Any missing person report?" the lawyer asked.

"None matching his description," the detective answered, "I check every time a new one comes in, just in case."

"She must know something about who he was," the lawyer said, "If I went missing my wife would have a bulletin out within a couple hours."

"My ex would have put out a bulletin to let the world know that I had been arrested," the detective said.

The men were quiet again. The mower had stopped, but the birds were still chirping. A burst of wind tugged at their jackets and rearranged the leaves. It went passed and was gone.

"I thought he might fight longer," the detective said, "It was almost like he gave up the minute he was arrested and yet there was this air that said that no one could touch him. I thought he would come up with some evidence that would create at least reasonable doubt with the jury."

"He didn't have anything to refute any of the evidence," the lawyer said, "Then the prosecution had the video and I knew we had lost any rapport we had with the jury. The video was pretty damning."

"We were lucky to get it," the detective said, "Twenty minutes later and we would not have gotten it. But you could have appealed the death penalty."

"He called it a waste of time," the lawyer replied, "He didn't see any point in it, despite what I said. For someone who was not ready to die, he was willing to be killed. Do you ever figure out who Jane Doe was?"

"The woman's name was Sheryl Kinsley. Her mother came forward after we put out the picture of what she might have looked like," the detective answered, "Apparently they had a fight and had not been talking to each other so she didn't know her daughter was missing. Now she is dealing with the guilt of not being there for her daughter. I don't think it would have made any difference, aside from knowing that her daughter had died in the most horrible manner several years earlier. I'm not sure which is worse."

"I think all the women who came into John's life became a victim to him," the lawyer said, "His wife may have no idea what happened to him. Sheryl was killed by him. Melissa thought she could blackmail him and was killed instead. Then there are any number of women, who he had affairs with. That makes a lot of victims."

"And yet I can't feel sympathy for most of them," the detective said, "Each one chose to become his victim. Although he did succeed at one thing that may or may not be a good thing."

"What is that?" the lawyer asked.

"His wife will never be bothered by law enforcement," the detective said, "or anyone else."

"True," the lawyer said.

"Come on, I'll buy you a coffee before we both have to get back to work," the detective said as he started to turn away from the grave stone.

"Sure," the lawyer said. He didn't turn. The detective waited for him. The birds had flown off with the gust of wind, but the mower could be heard again.

"I still wonder who he was," the lawyer said before turning.

# ABOUT THE AUTHOR

Heather Mantler is a lover of fairy tales and fables. Her home town is Prince George, British Columbia. Heather is always working on another story as she hopes to finish every story idea that she has ever written down. She was a nominee for the fiction category of the 2012 Prince George Regional Arts and Cultural Awards and short listed for the 2013 John Harris Fiction Awards. Her blog is heathersdomain.wordpress.com. Heather encourages her readers to post reviews on Good Reads and Amazon.

Other Works Published By Lit-N-Laughter
Math Troubles by Rosalyn Marie Francis
The Prince and the Rogue by Thomas Merritt
Man or Monkey by Rosalyn Marie Francis
The Magic of Serran by Frances Mantler
Dragons in Winter by multiple writers
Mythology Anthology by multiple writers
Down the Garden Path by Colleen Price